BILL NYE
the Science Guy's®

GREAT BIG BOOK of TINY
GERMS

With additional writing by
Kathleen W. Zoehfeld

Illustrated by
Bryn Barnard

Hyperion Books for Children • New York

Printed in Hong Kong
Jacket and book design by Angela Corbo Gier
First Edition
1 3 5 7 9 10 8 6 4 2
Library of Congress Cataloging-in-Publication Data on file
ISBN 0-7868-0543-9 (trade ed.)
Reinforced binding

Visit www.hyperionbooksforchildren.com

My mom helped me get this far. My family still jokes about her saying, "Wash
your hands; you've been to that dirty _____!" The blank could be "bus stop,"
"store," "soccer field," or "zoo." My dad taught us the importance of staying
clean while you're camping. So, this book is for my mother and father.
They kept me healthy as a kid, taught me to fight germs as a grown-up, and
inspired me to write a big book about those tiny germs. —B.N.

Science

CONTENTS

We're Outnumbered!. **4**

TRY THIS:
Grow your own germs that you can see
without a microscope! **7**

BACTERIA
They're Old and Tough. **8**

TRY THIS:
Find out how chemicals go in
and out of cells. **11**

VIRUSES
The Enemy That Gets Within. **12**

TRY THIS:
Pass a virus into a balloon
without bursting it. **15**

Germs Get Around!. **16**

TRY THIS:
See how quickly germs can reproduce. **19**

Germs Attack; We Fight Back **20**

TRY THIS:
Create your own germ-free preservatives. . . . **21**

The Immune System. **22**

TRY THIS:
Witness how alcohol kills germs. **25**

The History of Germs & Humans—
Pox, Plagues, and Little Demons. . . **26**

TRY THIS:
Use glitter to see how germs
get passed around. **29**

How Were Germs Discovered?. . . . **30**

TRY THIS:
Make your own microscope. **33**

What's in a Vaccination? **34**

TRY THIS:
Project live cells on your wall! **37**

Antibiotics **38**

TRY THIS:
Find out how your body keeps germs out. . . . **41**

HIV and AIDS. **42**

TRY THIS:
Reproduce Louis Pasteur's original experiment. **43**

Keeping Safe and Germ Free. **44**

TRY THIS:
Understand how germs grow. **47**

GERMS
We Love Them; We Hate Them . . . **48**

E. coli

WE'RE OUTNUMBERED!

There are trillions and trillions of them! They are everywhere, but you can't see them. They're in the air you breathe, in the water you drink, and in the soil under your feet. They're on plants and on animals. They're on your hair and skin. They're even in your mouth, and deep in your stomach and intestines. They're on the food you eat and on everything you touch! Some of them help you stay healthy, but now and then some of them make you sick. They're the tiniest organisms on Earth, and there are more of them than all other living things combined.

CHECK IT
OUT!

We've identified at least 300,000 different types of bacteria and about 5,000 viruses. There must still be thousands and thousands more to be discovered.

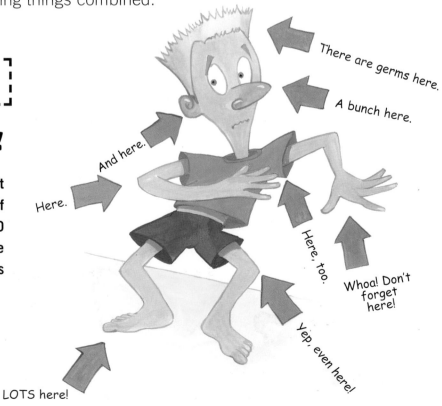

There are germs here.

A bunch here.

And here.

Here.

Here, too.

Whoa! Don't forget here!

Yep, even here!

LOTS here!

Germs are easy to forget about until you feel sick. You wake up one morning, and your body aches all over. You have a fever and chills. Maybe you have a sore throat or a cough. You know what's happened—you've caught a germ. Well, really, a germ has caught you.

When you get sick, you've been attacked by either a virus or a bacterium [back-TEER-ee-um]. If there are more than one, we call them bacteria [back-TEER-ee-uh]. A certain type of bacterium can give you strep throat. That's *streptococcus* [strep-tuh-KACK-us]. You may have had a staph infection— that's *staphylococcus* [staf-fill-uh-KACK-us]. Different kinds of viruses can give you a cold or the flu. Nearly every illness you can think of is brought on by bacteria or viruses, and they're much, much smaller than you can see.

None of us would be here if our bodies didn't fight germs. You may not feel it, but your body fights germs nonstop. When germs mount a strong attack, you get sick. Because your body fights back after a few days of rest, you almost always feel better. You fought and killed the germs that invaded your body.

HOW SMALL ARE THEY?

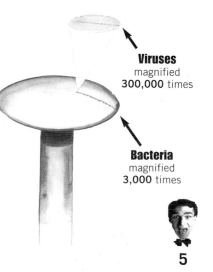

ACTUAL PIN SIZE

BACTERIA are so tiny that a thousand of them could fit side by side across the head of a pin. We measure distances that small in millionths of a meter, or micrometers [MIKE-roh-mee-terz]. For short, micrometers are sometimes called microns [MIKE-rahnz]. Many bacteria are only about one micron across.

VIRUSES are even tinier than bacteria. They have to be measured in nanometers [NANN-oh-meet-erz]— billionths of meters. The virus that causes the flu is about 100 nanometers across. You could get 10,000 of them lined up across the head of that pin.

Viruses
magnified
300,000 times

Bacteria
magnified
3,000 times

5

So, You Want to Stay Healthy Staying healthy takes energy—just like running, swimming, and thinking. Only, all the action is going on inside you. The best way to avoid getting sick is to exercise, eat nutritious food, and get plenty of rest every day. That helps your body stay ready and able to fight germs.

Humans have been fighting germs ever since there have been humans. Many of the germs that make us sick come from the things we touch with our hands. They get inside our bodies when we touch our mouths, noses, and eyes.

So, after playing, after petting your pets, after you poop or pee—wash your hands. Before you eat, always wash your hands, with plenty of soap and warm water. And don't rush it! Those germs stick to soap and water and then get carried away—off your hands and down the drain.

If you do get sick, help keep other people from catching your germs: cover your mouth when you cough or sneeze. If you don't have a tissue at hand, it's best to sneeze into your sleeve to keep germs off your hand. Use a clean tissue when you blow your nose. And then wash your hands!

TRY THIS!

THE QUESTION:
How can we grow germs to study them?

HERE'S WHAT YOU NEED:
any kind of bouillon cubes or powder · sugar · 1 envelope of gelatin
5 foil muffin cups (labeled 1 through 5) · a regular saucepan · water

1. In a pan, mix 15 milliliters (1 cube or 1 teaspoon) bouillon, 30 ml (2 teaspoons) sugar, 250 ml (1 cup) water, and 1 envelope of gelatin.

2. Bring mixture to a boil.

3. Divide it evenly among the five foil muffin cups.

4. Cover each cup with foil and let them all cool in the refrigerator.

5. When they're solid, do the following:

Cup 1: Touch with your finger.

Cup 2: Touch to a light switch.

Cup 3: Leave out for 15 minutes.

Cup 4: Wash your hands, then touch.

Cup 5: Leave covered.

Cup 1

Cup 2

Cup 3

6. Put cups in a warm place for two or three days, then observe. What happened? Are they the same? Or are they different? Why do you think you got these results?

Cup 4

Cup 5

Germs that land on the nutrients in the cups grow and multiply, making colonies big enough to see without a microscope.

Bacteria
They're Old and Tough

Bacteria are just about the most uncomplicated living things on Earth. They can survive in almost any environment you can imagine: from bitterly cold ice sheets to boiling hot springs, from the deepest parts of the ocean to the thin, thin air over 30 kilometers (20 miles) above the Earth's surface. They're everywhere.

Bacteria have their insides held within a wall or membrane [MEM-brain]. Each bacterium is separate; each has just one single cell [SELL], like separate houses on a street or separate eggs in a carton.

If you break open an egg, you'll find a yellow ball. That's the yolk. The yolk is the center structure, or nucleus [NOO-klee-iss], of an egg cell. When we talk about more than one nucleus, we say nuclei [NOO-klee-eye]. Just like those of chickens, our human cells have nuclei. So do plant cells, fungus cells, and many of the cells of microscopic creatures. But bacteria cells don't have nuclei. Their insides float around inside their membrane. Living things that have tiny structures like nuclei in each of their cells are called eukaryotes [yoo-CARE-ee-oats]. The name comes from Greek words that mean "having nuts." Organisms with cells that don't have nuclei are called prokaryotes [pro-CARE-ee-oats]. That name is Greek for "before nuts." Bacteria are prokaryotes. You and I are eukaryotes.

A REALLY CLOSE LOOK!
UP CLOSE AND PERSONAL WITH A PROKARYOTE

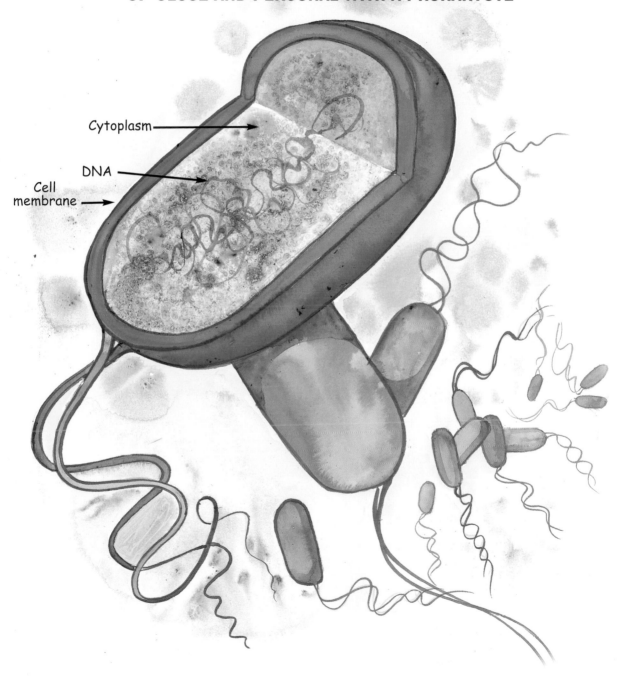

Cytoplasm

DNA

Cell membrane

How to Eat Without a Mouth: Lessons from an Experienced Bacterium

Many types of bacteria are expert food finders. *Escherichia coli*, or *E. coli*, a bacterium found in our intestines, has minute "nose spots" that help it sniff out food. Once E. coli finds some food, the bacterium can absorb it through its cell wall. If the substance is too large to be absorbed, the bacterium can secrete special chemicals to break down the substance before taking it in. As a bacterium digests its food, wastes form inside, and the bacterium passes the wastes right out through the same cell wall.

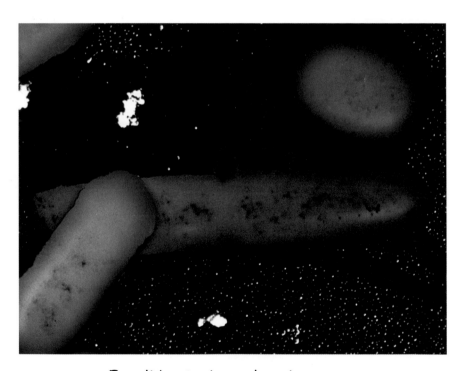

E. coli bacteria exchanging genes

CHECK IT

OUT!

Bacterial cells are simple structures. Cells in your body, and in animals and plants, have a nucleus where their DNA is held. Bacterial cells have no nucleus.

TRY THIS!

THE QUESTION:

How can chemicals pass in and out of a cell?

HERE'S WHAT YOU NEED:

liquid vanilla extract • a spoon • a balloon

1. Pour a very small amount of vanilla extract into the spoon, and set the spoon down on a countertop or table.

2. Using two fingers of one hand, stretch the neck of the balloon so that it's open as wide as possible.

3. Pour the vanilla from the spoon into the balloon.

4. Blow the balloon up.

5. Smell the balloon.

Vanilla molecules have passed right through the balloon like molecules passing through a cell wall.

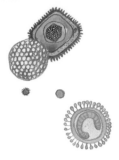

Avian flu virus

Viruses
The Enemy That Gets Within

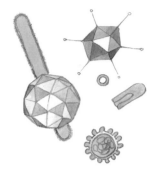

Viruses are organized packets of chemicals that use other organisms to help them make copies of themselves—to reproduce. It's hard to say whether or not viruses are living things. They can exist for years and years without doing anything. They don't need to move, eat, drink, or even breathe. Viruses are tiny and sturdy; they can endure in almost any environment on Earth. Some can even float around for centuries on specks of dust in outer space!

Viruses are made of just a few chemicals. They have a thin coat of protein around a core of DNA (deoxyribonucleic acid) or RNA (ribonucleic acid). While proteins give living things their structure, DNA and RNA molecules carry nothing but information, like a recipe. In the case of viruses, the recipe contains the information necessary for a virus to make almost perfect copies of itself. That is, once it attaches to a host cell. Some types of viruses need plant host cells; others need animal or human host cells.

Viruses come in a wide variety of shapes—spheres, rods, and even tiny bullets. Others are like microscopic corkscrews. The viruses that cause a certain type of pneumonia are little spheres with exactly twenty triangular faces attached edge to edge, like panels on soccer balls. The measles virus is studded with spikes. A virus's outer protein coat is specially shaped and chemically suited to attach itself to its host cell, the cell it attacks. Once it attaches itself, a virus gets down to work burrowing into the host cell and using that cell to make replicas of itself. Viruses are made to invade.

Bacteriophage Attack! A virus that attacks a bacterium is called a bacteriophage [bak-TEER-ee-uh-fayj], a "bacterium eater." It's a virus with a six-sided head and a spiral tail that has six spindly fibers sticking out near the end. When a phage finds the right kind of bacterium, it uses its tail fibers to attach itself. Chemicals from its tail dissolve a hole in the bacterium's cell wall. The phage squeezes its tail down like a spring and injects the DNA from its head into the bacterium. The phage's DNA then takes over the host bacterium, instructing it to make hundreds of copies of the phage until the bacterium explodes. The new phages spread out in search of more bacteria to take over.

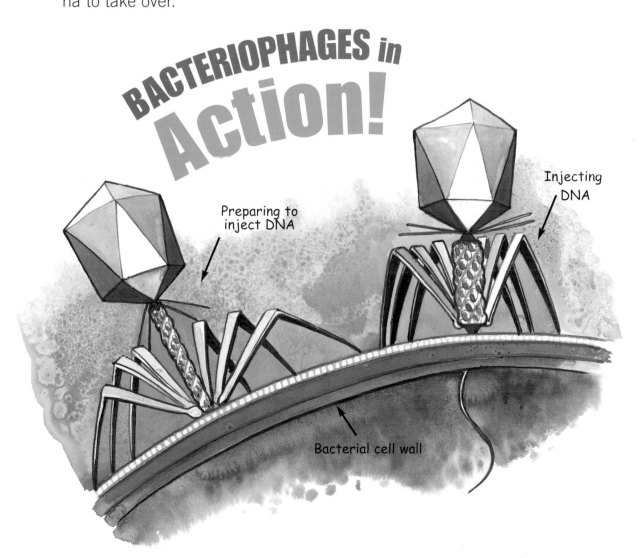

BACTERIOPHAGES in Action!

Preparing to inject DNA

Injecting DNA

Bacterial cell wall

THE HANDY "LIVING OR NONLIVING?" CHECKLIST OF SCIENCE

DOES IT eat? ✓

DOES IT grow? ✓

DOES IT give off waste? ✓

DOES IT reproduce? ✓

If the answer to these questions is "yes," then you are definitely looking at a living thing. But viruses don't exactly fit. They do not eat, but they must use energy. They don't grow, exactly. They make copies or "replicate" themselves. They don't give off waste, but as they replicate, they fall apart. So are they living or nonliving? It's hard to know. Viruses are viruses.

Viral REPLICATION!

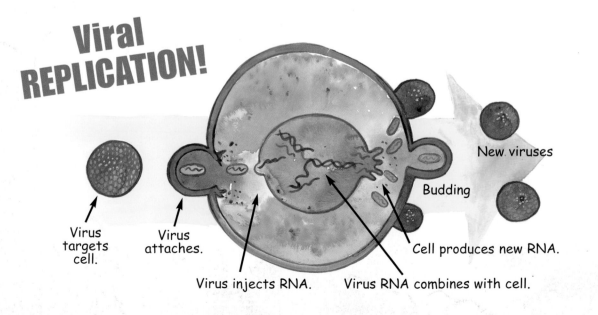

Virus targets cell.

Virus attaches.

Virus injects RNA.

Virus RNA combines with cell.

Cell produces new RNA.

New viruses

Budding

TRY THIS!

THE QUESTION:

How does a bacteriophage get into a cell without destroying it?

HERE'S WHAT YOU NEED:

a balloon • a little cooking oil • a wooden skewer or long toothpick

1. Inflate your balloon and tie it closed.

2. Pour some oil into a small container, like the cap for the oil bottle.

3. Wet the tip of the wooden skewer with oil.

4. Gently poke the wooden skewer into the inflated balloon, aiming for an area where the balloon is thick, such as near the knot or near the top.

The balloon doesn't pop because the molecules of rubber push apart from one another without tearing the surface. The same thing happens when the end of a virus pierces the wall of a bacterium. The bacterium holds together long enough for the virus to take over.

GERMS GET AROUND!

Germs can't walk, run, or fly—yet they are constantly on the move. Germs are the smallest living things—yet, in a way, they are the most powerful organisms on Earth. In a matter of weeks, a flu virus in one country can travel around the world, infecting millions of people, making them miserable—coughing, sneezing, and feverishly aching.

How do they do it? For one thing, germs can multiply quickly. Once it has invaded a host cell, one tiny virus can create hundreds of copies of itself in a matter of hours. The exhausted host cell bursts, sending those hundreds out to invade other host cells.

In 1917, the Spanish flu killed 25 million people in one winter—four months. Twenty-five million people were killed in World War I, but that took four years. So what's more powerful, two armies or one germ?

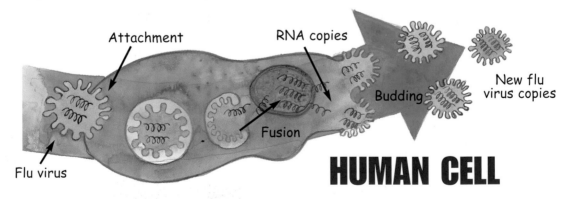

Attachment · RNA copies · Fusion · Budding · New flu virus copies · Flu virus

HUMAN CELL

CHECK IT
SOAP
OUT!

One bacterium could, in about three days, produce enough new bacteria to equal the mass of the entire Earth. What keeps that from happening is that a lot of things fight bacteria, including you and me.

Do the math, and you can see how quickly one virus can turn into a million. Suppose there is a type of virus that makes 100 copies of itself in a host cell before the cell bursts:

1 virus in 1 host cell: 1 x 100 = 100 viruses

100 new viruses move into 100 host cells: 100 x 100 = 10,000 viruses

10,000 new viruses move into 10,000 host cells:
10,000 x 10,000 = 1,000,000 viruses in a few hours!

Go ahead. You **do the math.**

Bacteria Multiply by Dividing Viruses are replicated inside host cells. Most bacteria reproduce by just dividing themselves in two. We call that process binary fission [BYE-nuh-ree FISH-un]. Binary means "two." And fission means "splitting."

First the bacterium makes a copy of its own genetic information, its own DNA. Then it forms a cross-wall, a wall through its own middle. The cross-wall splits into two layers, and two new bacteria are created, each containing one copy of the DNA strands.

Some bacteria can divide themselves as fast as every twenty minutes.

Do the math, and you'll see how one bacterium can produce millions.

1 bacterium becomes 2. 2 divide to become 4.
4 become 8. 8 become 16.
16 become 32. 32 become 64. 64 become 128.

After eight binary fissions, there will be 256 bacteria. Dividing every twenty minutes, there will be more than a million of them in a matter of hours.

Whoa!

Germs Hitch a Ride Germs are parasites [PAIR-uh-sites]. They're organisms that, to get around, live in or on other living things. The word *parasite* comes from Greek words that mean "eating at the same table." Germs use the bodies of their hosts to live.

You've probably caught a cold from someone in school or in your family. The germ traveled from one person to another. We say that these germs cause communicable [kuh-MYOON-ih-kuh-bull] diseases. That word comes from the same root as communicate. It describes the way germs that cause disease can spread from one person to many others. Germs can spread from animals to animals, and even from animals to humans once in a while. Sometimes insects, such as mosquitoes and fleas, carry germs from the blood of animals or people and pass them on to thousands of others when they bite people and animals to feed on their blood.

Millions of particles of cold viruses ride in the little droplets of moisture that get sprayed when you sneeze. A sneeze travels out of your lungs at about 150 kilometers (almost 100 miles) per hour. That's one big, bad blast of germs!

TRY THIS!

THE QUESTION:
What happens when germs divide?

HERE'S WHAT YOU NEED:
a sheet of paper • a pencil with an eraser • an ink pad

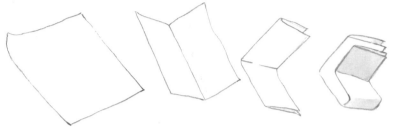

1. Fold the paper in half three times, once along the length, then twice along the width, so that you have eight spaces.

2. Touch the pencil eraser to the ink pad and then to the paper, making one "germ dot."

3. Make two dots in the second box.

4. Then make four dots in the third, eight dots in the fourth, and so on.

You can see that if the eraser circles were germs with room to multiply, it wouldn't take long for the world to be covered with pencil-eraser circles. Germs don't take over the world by doubling, though, because they can't get enough nutrients.

GERMS ATTACK
We Fight Back

Your body is a champion germ fighter. When it comes to keeping germs out, your skin is like a suit of armor. The outer surface of your skin may feel soft and alive, but actually, what you see and feel is a thin layer of dead skin cells. That outer layer of you is called the epidermis [ep-ih-DERM-iss]. It is a tough barrier against germs.

If you cut or scrape your skin, wash the area well to slide germs off. Cover the cut with a very clean bandage to keep germs out. A cut or scrape can be like an open door; germs can tumble right into your body.

In fact, anywhere skin is not covering you, there are germ invaders trying to get in. The moist passages of your nose produce mucus, the gooey fluid in your nose. The wet lining is sticky, so it filters the air you breathe and traps germs before they get too far.

Once in a while, dust and germs get past your nose and make their way down your windpipe, or trachea [TRAY-kee-uh], to your bronchial [BRON-kee-ul] tubes—the tubes that spread air out in your lungs. Tiny hairlike structures in your trachea and bronchial tubes, called cilia [SILL-ee-uh], whip and wave around all the time. They're like tiny brushes swishing dust and germs back up into your throat where you can swallow them. Then the germs go down to your stomach, where digestive acids dissolve them.

The salty tears that keep your eyes moist are natural germ killers. And the watery saliva in your mouth can break up some germs, too. But sometimes, in spite of all its natural defenses, a few germs find their way in. When germs get in, your internal bodyguards go to work.

TRY THIS!

THE QUESTION:

How do we keep germs from invading our food?

HERE'S WHAT YOU NEED:

a pot and a stove • water • any vegetable • four clean glasses
salt • sugar • vinegar • labels of your own design

1. On the stove, heat some water, and boil or steam any type of vegetable. (Ask an adult to help you with this.)

2. Pour the water from the pot of vegetables into the four glasses.

3. In the first glass, mix in 2½ milliliters (½ teaspoon) of salt, and label the glass.

4. In the second glass, mix in 5 ml of sugar, and label it.

5. In the third glass, mix in 5 ml of vinegar, and label it.

6. Leave the fourth glass alone, and label it.

7. Set these in a warm place for a few days.

The glass with nothing added will turn cloudy first, because microorganisms start growing in the vegetable water. The food chemicals you added to the other three keep the water out of balance for microbes. It takes much longer for them to grow into a colony big enough to see. That's why we use salt to preserve pickles and sugar to preserve jelly and jam, and why vinegar doesn't have to be refrigerated.

White blood cells

The Immune System

OUR HERO
THE WHITE BLOOD CELL

The way you and I fight germs is with special cells in our bloodstream that look white or clear under a microscope. We call them leukocytes [LOO-koh-sites], which means "white blood cells."

Some common cold viruses make their way through the mucus in your nose. They invade cells and the battle begins. The viruses replicate quickly. They take over cell after cell. Many of your inner nose cells die!

VIRUSES ATTACK WE FIGHT BACK!

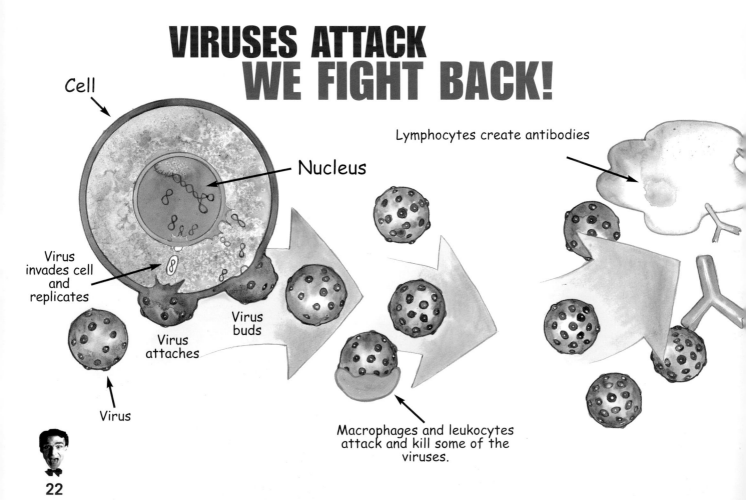

Cell

Nucleus

Lymphocytes create antibodies

Virus invades cell and replicates

Virus attaches

Virus buds

Virus

Macrophages and leukocytes attack and kill some of the viruses.

The cells under attack send out special chemicals that tell your body, *We need help!* The germs irritate your nose to make you drip and sneeze, spreading germs to other people. At the same time, dripping and sneezing help drive germs out of your body. Like good soldiers on horseback, there are white blood cells always riding on patrol in the flow of your bloodstream. They rush to the area. Macrophages **[MAK-roh-fay-jiz]** (their name means "big eaters") and white blood cells kill germs by wrapping themselves around the bacteria and dissolving them or making them explode.

At the same time, special protein molecules in our blood, called *antibodies* **(AN-tee-baw-dees)**, are formed. Antibodies are produced by a type of leukocyte called a lymphocyte **[LIM-foh-site]**. Antibodies are designed to recognize the patterns of chemicals on the outside of different types of invading germs. When a certain type of cold virus invades, antibodies that recognize those cold viruses attach themselves to the surface of each one.

An antibody is like a bright signal flag that your body places on each germ, telling your white blood cells, "Attack this!" More white blood cells hurry in and kill the marked germs.

Once a particular germ has invaded your body, your body's immune system keeps a protein record of that germ. Next time that type of germ sneaks in, your body is able to produce and send out antibodies against it very quickly, before it can make you sick. You have developed an immunity **[ih-MYOON-ih-tee]** to that type of germ.

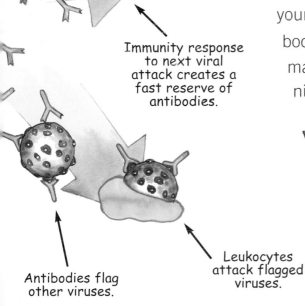

Immunity response to next viral attack creates a fast reserve of antibodies.

Antibodies flag other viruses.

Leukocytes attack flagged viruses.

Mutations What makes germs so tricky is that they don't stay the same. Try carefully printing your name. Then copy it exactly. The copies won't be identical to the first one. Look closely: even photocopies aren't exact copies. The same is true for bacteria and viruses. The bacteria in each new generation are slightly different from earlier ones. This process is called mutation [myoo-TAY-shun]. We say that germs mutate [MYOO-tayt]. Mutation turns out to be a great thing for viruses and bacteria, but not so great for us.

If you have leukocytes and antibodies that are ready to fight one kind of germ, they may not be able to find and fight these new next-generation germs. This is a big reason why we have gotten colds and the flu for thousands and thousands of years. The viruses that cause colds are always changing. It's been going on since the beginning of life on Earth. We have to have evolving immune systems to keep up with the new germs coming along to attack us.

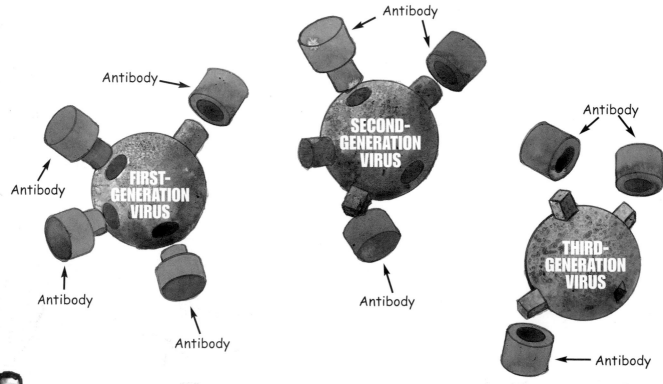

24

TRY THIS!

THE QUESTION:

How does alcohol kill germs?

HERE'S WHAT YOU NEED:

water • rubbing (isopropyl) alcohol
waxed paper • a toothpick

1. Sprinkle a few drops of water onto a sheet of waxcd paper.

2. Pour some alcohol into a very small dish; the top of the alcohol bottle is often perfect for this.

3. Break the tip of the toothpick, so that the end has tiny bristles.

4. Touch the edge of one of the droplets of water with the bristly tip of the toothpick.

5. Dip the toothpick in the alcohol, and touch a droplet of water again.

Water molecules stick to each other. That's how the water droplets hold their shape. Alcohol molecules pull on water molecules almost in the same way magnets pull on metals. When alcohol flows over a germ, the water in the germ gets pulled out by chemical force. The germ's cell wall is disrupted. This is why we use alcohol to disinfect cuts and the surface of our skin. It kills germs.

Clusters of polio virus

The History of
Germs & Humans
Pox, Plagues, and Little Demons

Today, germs make a lot of us sick. But not so long ago, countless people, especially children, died from diseases caused by germs. Most of the nightmarish diseases that our ancestors suffered from can now be prevented or cured. In fact, we hardly even think about most of them anymore.

Consider some of the diseases that gave our ancestors great misery. Diphtheria **[diff-THEER-ee-uh]** causes people's throats to swell so terribly that they close up and the sufferers cannot breathe. Smallpox, one of the most deadly diseases in human history, causes fever and terrible skin rashes. Polio attacks the spinal cord and can cause people's arms and legs to be permanently paralyzed. And there are diseases that cause even more misery.

These diseases spread quickly. In the old days, they could wipe out whole towns and cities. In the 1300s, the bubonic plague **[byoo-BON-ick PLAYG]**, or "Black Death," killed off more than one third of all the people in Europe. Up to 30 million people died. The symptoms were so creepy many people thought that demons had taken over people's bodies, making them sick. Some thought the disease was God's punishment for evil deeds. Some blamed it on spooky vapors that were thought to seep out of the ground into the air. The word bubonic refers to horrible swelling sores called buboes **[BYOO-bohz]** that infected people get.

We know now that the bubonic plague is caused by a bacterium. It lives in blood. It's spread by fleas that have been living on infected rats or other animals. By keeping rats away from places where humans lived, people could keep the disease under control.

It's hard to believe, but for thousands, perhaps millions, of years, no one figured out what really caused the bubonic plague or any other disease, or how to stop their deadly spread. People tried all kinds of remedies to keep disease away—drinking witches' brews, wearing masks, building houses that faced away from the "evil" winds. Of course, none of these had any real effect. Maybe they made people feel safe.

It's cherry flavored.

CHECK IT SOAP OUT!

The mummy of Ramses V, one of the pharaohs of ancient Egypt, shows signs of smallpox infection. Ramses V died in 1156 B.C. Today, smallpox has been almost completely wiped out. In fact, there are only a few remaining smallpox germs. They are stored in test tubes, frozen in liquid nitrogen, and guarded around the clock to prevent anyone from getting to them. If someone captured a sample of smallpox, he or she could start a terrible epidemic.

Ring Around the Rosy Remember that nursery rhyme? It comes from the days of the Black Death, when many people thought—or hoped—that a fresh bouquet of flowers ("posies") might ward off the deadly disease. People still bring flowers to loved ones who are sick. And it still does cheer us up.

TRY THIS!

THE QUESTION:

How do germs pass from person to person?

HERE'S WHAT YOU NEED:

any type of glitter

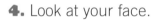

1. Sprinkle just a few flakes of glitter into your hand.
2. Shake hands with people.
3. Look at your friends' hands near a bright light.
4. Look at your face.

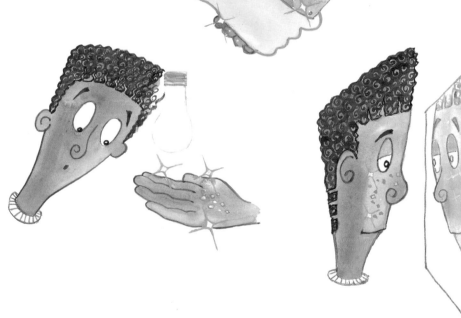

The sparkles stick to us like germs. The shiny surfaces of the glitter let us see how easily they get around. If some get on your or your friends' faces, it just shows how often we touch our faces without thinking about it.

How Were
Germs Discovered?

For most of human history, people had no idea that germs even existed. That's not surprising, since we can't see germs without a microscope, and microscopes were not invented until the 1600s.

The first microscopes were not very strong or clear. But in the 1670s, Antoni van Leeuwenhoek **[LAY-ven-hook]**, a cloth merchant and avid lensmaker from Holland, created a microscope with a lens so fine it could magnify objects by up to 200 times.

Van Leeuwenhoek lookcd at all kinds of things with his new microscope. He even looked at the plaque on his own teeth, and he observed that there were "many small living animalcules" in it. Those "animalcules" were bacteria, and van Leeuwenhoek was the first person to see them. When he drank very hot liquids, he noticed that there were suddenly fewer of them.

Sample holder

Focus Knob

Lens

Positioner

Yikes!

30

Still, it took scientists a long time to convince people that germs existed—about two hundred years. Can you imagine? Scientists were looking at the animalcules, but no one connected them to sicknesses for another two centuries.

In the late 1800s, people built microscopes strong enough to allow them to see many bacteria clearly. With time and patience French scientist Louis Pasteur [pas-TYER], Robert Koch [KOKE], and other scientists identified many types of germs. Louis Pasteur designed and carried out very careful experiments that proved once and for all that humankind's most harmful diseases were caused by germs. Eventually scientists were able to figure out which germs caused which diseases. They experimented with ways of preventing some of those awful afflictions.

Pretty cool, huh?

And the Even Tinier Viruses? Many scientists long believed that organisms smaller than bacteria must exist. But no one saw viruses until the 1930s, when the first electron microscopes, which used beams of electrons instead of beams of light, were designed. At last, different types of viruses could be seen and identified.

Yep!

Does this machine help us see germs?

CHECK IT

OUT!

The virus that causes yellow fever is so small 40,000 of them would fit inside an average bacterium. The smallpox virus is one of the largest viruses. It would take about four of them to equal the size of a small bacterium.

TRY THIS!

THE QUESTION:

How does a microscope work?

HERE'S WHAT YOU NEED:

a small piece of thin cardboard, like a piece of a cereal box
a hole punch or scissors • plastic wrap • adhesive tape • water

1. Cut a strip of cardboard about 3 centimeters wide and 10 cm long.

2. Punch a single hole at a spot about 1 cm from one end.

3. Cut a square piece of plastic wrap 2 cm by 2 cm.

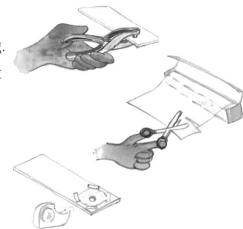

4. Tape it to the cardboard so that it covers the hole.

5. Push the plastic with your fingertip so that it forms a small well or dent.

6. Put the smallest drop of water you can in the well.

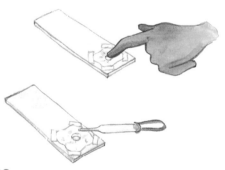

7. Look at the number at the bottom of this page through it; it will be magnified.

Magnifying lenses make light change direction by directing it through curved surfaces. The smaller the droplet, the more it magnifies. Bigger droplets magnify less, but they let more light through.

Look here!

What's *in* A Vaccination?

In 1796, an English doctor named Edward Jenner observed that milkmaids and farmers who caught a mild rash called cowpox from their cows never seemed to get infected with smallpox. So he decided to perform a dangerous experiment.

He wondered what would happen if he infected a person with cowpox on purpose. Would the cowpox infection somehow protect that person from deadly smallpox? He took some of the oozing fluid from a milkmaid's cowpox rash, made two small cuts on a young boy's arm, and let the fluid pass through the cuts into the boy's bloodstream. Soon the boy caught cowpox but got over it. Six weeks later, Dr. Jenner exposed the boy to smallpox—and he stayed healthy.

Nowadays, if a doctor were to expose someone deliberately to a deadly disease, people might think he was crazy. Other doctors who knew Jenner were very critical of his methods. Nevertheless, his experiment proved that getting a mild case of cowpox could prevent smallpox.

How We Got the Name The medical name for cowpox is *Vaccinia* (vak-SINN-ee-uh). In honor of Jenner's process of giving people cowpox to prevent smallpox, Pasteur called his process of protecting people from a deadly germ by exposing them to a weakened form of that germ a vaccination. And that's what we still call the "shots" we get to protect us from many different diseases today.

Jenner knew his experiment had worked, but he did not know exactly why it had worked. Until Louis Pasteur began his research, no one understood that germs caused disease.

Vacca means "cow" in Latin.

In the 1880s, in one of his most famous experiments, Pasteur isolated a type of bacterium that seemed to be the cause of anthrax, a killer disease in sheep. He grew colonies of pure anthrax bacteria in his laboratory. Building on Jenner's work, Pasteur worked out a method of first weakening the bacteria and then introducing the weakened bacteria into the sheep's blood.

Sheep exposed to the weakened bacteria did not die. Not only that, they became immune to anthrax.

Pasteur went on to discover the way to prevent people from getting the disease rabies, by exposing them to rabies germs in a weakened form. Rabies most often affects animals. It makes them so crazy they go around biting other animals and spreading the disease. A human who gets bitten by a rabid animal will almost certainly die if he or she hasn't had a rabies vaccination. The vaccine used today is very similar to the one developed by Pasteur.

In the twenty-first century, most children visit their doctors regularly to get vaccinations against measles, mumps, diphtheria, tetanus, polio, whooping cough, chicken pox, smallpox, and other diseases. Each year, I get a flu shot. That hypodermic needle may hurt a bit, but consider the consequences of not getting your shots!

Most vaccinations are made up of weakened germs that go through a needle, into your skin, and then into your bloodstream. Your white blood cells check out those germs and make antibodies against them. Later on, if you're exposed to the full-strength germ, your body has the ability to recognize it right away and attack it. Your immune system makes enough antibodies to fight off the germs before they make you sick.

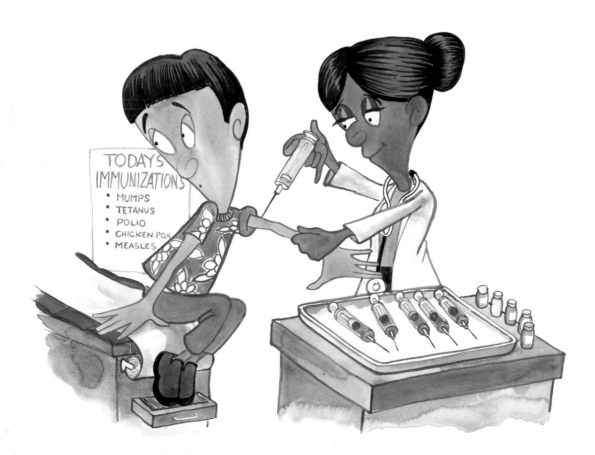

TODAY'S IMMUNIZATIONS
- MUMPS
- TETANUS
- POLIO
- CHICKEN POX
- MEASLES

TRY THIS!

THE QUESTION:

How can we see cells?

HERE'S WHAT YOU NEED:

scissors • aluminum foil • a flashlight with strong batteries • a rubber band
a pin • tape • a piece of white paper • a sharp knife and a cutting board
a fresh onion • a small picture frame with a glass front

1. Cut or tear a piece of foil to fit over the lens of the flashlight, and attach it on with the rubber band.

2. In the center, poke the very tiniest hole you can with the pin.

3. Tape the paper to the back of a chair or to the wall.

4. Cut a slice of onion. (Ask an adult to help you.)

5. Separate the layers; peel off the thinnest layer of onion that you can, and lay it on the glass.

6. Hold the glass right up against the pinhole in the foil.

7. Move the light until you can see a pattern on the paper.

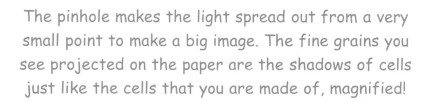

The pinhole makes the light spread out from a very small point to make a big image. The fine grains you see projected on the paper are the shadows of cells just like the cells that you are made of, magnified!

Penicillium fungus on bread

Antibiotics

I'm going to save the world!

Have you ever been very sick? Did you take an antibiotic drug? Antibiotics are special poisons that are created by living things. Penicillin comes from mold, a type of fungus called *penicillium notatum*. It makes a chemical that breaks down a bacterium's cell wall. By concentrating this special poison, we can use it to help us fight bacteria. We can have these antibiotic chemicals floating around inside us, and they will do us no harm. But when they encounter the right type of bacterium, they are poisonous to it. This works because the poison molecule has a very particular shape, and it only attacks a special type of molecule on the bacterium's cell wall. The wall falls apart, and the bacterium can't reproduce. Our white blood cells and macrophages absorb it and produce antibodies, which can attack and absorb even more.

Bacterium reproduces.

No Penicillin

Penicillin

Bacterium is unable to reproduce.

KA-POW!

Bacteriocins We fight bacteria; bacteria also fight bacteria. They use poisons or toxins called bacteriocins [bak-TEER-ee-oh-sinz]. One type of bacterium in your intestines produces lots of bacteriocin toxin. Another produces chemicals that resist that toxin. A third type is susceptible to the bacteriocin, but it reproduces so fast that the toxin producers can't get ahead. It's a microbial game of rock, paper, scissors! If we figure out how bacteria manufacture these toxins, it may be possible to come up with new ways to fight diseases.

Take the Right Drug for the Right Bug Antibiotics work only against bacteria. They have no effect at all on viruses—none. Viruses don't have cell walls to disrupt. So if you or someone in your family is sick with a virus, taking an antibiotic would be a waste of time. You might think that taking a drug that does nothing won't cause any trouble, but it does.

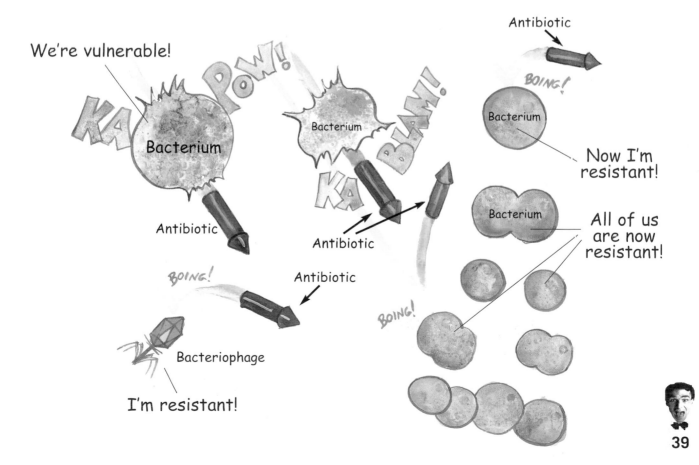

We're vulnerable!

Bacterium

Antibiotic

Bacterium

Antibiotic

BOING!

Bacteriophage

I'm resistant!

Antibiotic

BOING!

Bacterium

Now I'm resistant!

Bacterium

All of us are now resistant!

BOING!

All the time you're sick, bacteria are reproducing inside you. Some of them are different from the generation that produced them; they're mutating. So, as bacteria run into the antibiotic you've taken, the cell walls of most of them fall apart. But some of the bacteria survive. They happen to be resistant to the antibiotic. By taking an antibiotic when you have a virus, you are breeding antibiotic-resistant bacteria inside you. You're part of evolution.

When you sneeze and breathe, you're spreading these antibiotic-resistant bacteria all over the place, to live and grow inside the rest of us. So, don't take an antibiotic if it's the wrong drug for your bug. And always finish your course of antibiotics. Otherwise, the few bacteria that happen to be resistant to the drug you're taking will live and grow, and antibiotics won't work for any of us anymore.

CHECK IT OUT!

People exploring mud on the ocean floor may have found ancient oceanic fungi, which the germs that attack us land animals haven't encountered before. Some of those deep-sea fungis produce antibacterial chemicals that may destroy our germ enemies. Exploration of the enormous ocean floor may help us produce new antibiotics to fight tiny bacteria.

Antibiotic attacks bacteria.

Most die; resistant bacteria survive.

Resistant bacteria reproduce.

Next time, antibiotic fails.

TRY THIS!

THE QUESTION:

How can we keep germs from getting inside us?

HERE'S WHAT YOU NEED:

a paper towel • water • two plastic sandwich bags • dirt • two slices of bread

1. Tear the paper towel in half.
2. Get each piece wct, and put one piece in each plastic bag.
3. Rub your fingers in some dirt.
4. Touch your dirty fingers to one slice of bread.
5. Put that slice in one of the bags along with the wet towel. Close it tightly, either using a twist tie or its own zipper-style closure.
6. Wash your hands well, with soap and water—take a full minute.
7. Pick up the other slice of bread, and put it in the second bag. Seal it tightly as well.

You'll soon see mold growing on the dirty bread. Washing your hands takes away dirt and microscopic germs.

WANTED
DEAD (NOT ALIVE)

HIV

Red blood cells

HIV and AIDS

We fight germs with our white blood cells and the fluids that carry them. Together, they form our immune system, our best defense against germs. But there is a type of germ that doesn't attack just any old cell; it attacks the cells of our immune system. That's right. There are viruses that attack our white blood cells, destroying the cells we use to fight germs. One of them is the Human Immunodeficiency Virus, or HIV. It is devilish. It can take months or years to destroy a body's immune system. Then, all kinds of germs that you normally have no problem with make you very, very sick. The complex disease or condition caused by HIV is called Acquired Immunodeficiency Syndrome, or AIDS. So far, we don't have a vaccine or cure. Epidemiologists **[EPP-ih-dee-mee-ALL-uh-jists]**, scientists who study the spread of diseases, say that at least 30 million people are infected with HIV. You can't catch it by shaking hands or hugging or being near someone who's coughing or sneezing. It's trickier than that.

In a person who is infected, the virus hangs around where there are white blood cells, in their blood and other bodily fluids. The virus spreads from one person to another through close sexual contact. People who use illegal drugs and share hypodermic needles can pass the virus to one another through their needles. Sometimes a pregnant mother infected with HIV can pass the virus on to her unborn baby. There have been some cases of the virus passing in donated blood from infected, but seemingly healthy, people; now we have a way to test donated blood for the HIV, so this problem has become very, very rare.

TRY THIS!

THE QUESTION:

Why was Louis Pasteur so sure that germs were in the air?

HERE'S WHAT YOU NEED:

soap • some water • a clean plastic drinking water bottle with a push–pull closable cap • two bendable straws • bathtub (silicone) caulk a slice of bread • a paper towel • an oven

1. Wash your hands well.

2. Break the valve off the push–pull, closable part of the bottle cap. (Try tapping it with the bottom of a heavy skillet.)

3. Fit the long end of one of the bendable straws into the long end of the other straw. Then place one of the short ends through the hole in the bottle cap.

4. Use the caulk to seal the straw in the bottle cap and then seal the straws together. (Leave both ends open to the air.)

5. Let the caulk set overnight.

6. Tear a strip off the slice of bread and drop it into the bottle.

7. Tear the paper towel in half, get it wet, and drop it into the bottle.

8. Screw the top on snugly, and bend the straws so that they form a tube that comes up out of the bottle, down toward the table, and then back up again.

9. Place your bread bottle in a shallow pan of water. Turn oven to 75° Celsius (167° Fahrenheit) or to a similarly low setting, and put the pan and bottle in for at least an hour.

10. Remove the bottle from the oven, and set it aside in a warm area for a few days. Support the straws with a book if you need to.

11. After you've observed the bread, take the top off the bottle and set it aside for a few more days.

At first no mold grows in the bottle. There is hardly any airflow to carry germs up into the bottle to the bread. After you open the bottle, mold can get in and grow. This is what Louis Pasteur did, but he didn't have a century of science to help him know what to try.

Keeping Safe and Germ Free

It's hard to believe, but humans have been around for millions of years, and it wasn't until less than 150 years ago that people started to believe in germs. They may have noticed that keeping things clean helped keep you healthy, but they didn't know what you know.

It's hard to say it often enough: wash your hands!

Before people knew about germs, doctors at hospitals would treat sick people in one room and then operate on patients or deliver babies in another room, without washing their hands! People wondered why so many healthy mothers died after childbirth. They wondered why, after perfectly successful surgery, many patients became ill with fevers and never pulled through. It took a long time for scientists to convince doctors that their strong, surgically skilled hands were covered with disease-causing germs!

Today doctors scrub their hands thoroughly, then put on clean gloves and clothes before treating patients. Hospital work surfaces are kept clean and sanitary—free of germs.

Before people knew about germs, they had problems with food spoiling quickly, because of microorganisms at work. Louis Pasteur proved that a certain type of bacterium is responsible for turning milk sour. He experimented with heating milk to just the right temperature, long enough to kill the bacteria without making the milk fat separate. When he did that, the milk stayed sweet and fresh much longer. Almost all the milk we drink today is put through that same heating process. We call it pasteurization [pas-TYER-ih-ZAY-shun]. Ancient people knew that cooking makes food safe. Pasteur proved why. Cooking our food with heat kills the bacteria that may be in it. But if bacteria get into cooked foods as the foods cool off, you're back where you started. So cover those leftovers and get them into the fridge quick! The cold air of the refrigerator won't kill germs, but it greatly slows their growth and keeps your foods fresh for a few days. The colder air of the freezer will keep them even longer.

Got milk, Louis?

In the Kitchen, Work Safely You might eat meat every day. But juices from raw meats may contain bacteria that can make you very sick. After you place or slice meats on a cutting board or a plate, always wash and sanitize that surface before using it for other foods. Keep those other kitchen utensils sanitary, too. Germs don't survive in a clean kitchen!

Cheese or yogurt lactobacillus, madame?

Mmm, germy!

CHECK IT **OUT!**

Not all bacteria are bad. Sometimes we want bacteria in our food. Without bacteria, we would have no cheese or yogurt. These yummy foods are made with types of bacteria that are very good for you. There are more bacteria in your stomach than there are people on Earth. We all evolved together. We need each other.

Understand That Can! Cans keep food fresh for a long time, because the food is cooked in the can, and no air or bacteria can get in. Once in a while, though, bacteria accidentally get into the can with the food. This can lead to a dangerous disease called botulism [BOT-choo-lih-zum]. Botulinum bacteria give off a gas as they grow. The trapped gas will make the ends of the can bulge out. Never eat food from a bulging can! It's toxic.

TRY THIS!

THE QUESTION:
Why do we keep food in refrigerators?

HERE'S WHAT YOU NEED:
two clean 1-liter or 2-liter plastic soda bottles • warm water
two packets of yeast • sugar • two balloons

1. Fill the soda bottles halfway with warm water.
2. Pour a packet of yeast into each one.
3. Pour 15 milliliters (1 tablespoon) of sugar into each one.
4. Fit a balloon over the neck of each bottle.
5. Put one bottle in a warm place.
6. Put the other bottle in your refrigerator.

Yeast is a microorganism that we eat in bread. It gives off carbon dioxide. (The bubbles make the little pockets you see in a slice of bread.) When the yeast is kept cool, it can't grow very fast. Germs are the same way; that's why we keep food in the refrigerator.

GERMS
We LOVE Them
We Hate Them

Because germs affect us all every moment of every day, it is important to understand them. But since we only began to understand germs a few dozen years ago, there must be a great deal more we don't know about them, such as:

- **How will we come up with new vaccines to fight newly evolving bacteria?**

- **Can we figure out which germs are going to mutate and then get our bodies to create antibodies for the new germs before they start to infect anyone?**

- **Is there a way to make an "antivirotic" drug?**

- **Can we make a drug that fights more than one virus, like the viruses that cause the so-called common cold?**

- **Are there dangerous undiscovered germs that will come after us as the world's climate changes?**

Maybe you'll be the one who uncovers their next secret.

Germ Science Rules!